P9-DNN-508

2378

2223604

The Viking Press   New York

Arrow to the Sun

a Pueblo
Indian tale
adapted and
illustrated

by Gerald McDermott

LINTHICUM ELEMENTARY
SCHOOL LIBRARY

VIKING
Viking Penguin Inc.
A Division of Penguin Books USA Inc.
375 Hudson Street, New York, New York 10014
Penguin Books Ltd, 27 Wrights Lane, London W8 5TZ (Publishing & Editorial) and
Harmondsworth, Middlesex, England (Distribution & Warehouse)
Penguin Books Australia Ltd, Ringwood, Victoria, Australia
Penguin Books Canada Limited, 2801 John Street, Markham, Ontario, Canada L3R 1B4
Penguin Books (N.Z.) Ltd, 182-190 Wairau Road, Auckland 10, New Zealand

Copyright © Gerald McDermott, 1974
All rights reserved
First published in 1974 by The Viking Press
Published simultaneously in Canada
Printed in the United States of America
Set in Clarendon Book
20 19 18 17 16 15 14 13 12 11

Library of Congress Cataloging-in-Publication Data
McDermott, Gerald.   Arrow to the sun.
SUMMARY: An adaptation of the Pueblo Indian
myth which explains how the spirit of the
Lord of the Sun was brought to the world of men.
[1. Pueblo Indians—Legends] I. Title.
PZ8.1.M159A4   291.2' 12 [398.2] [E] 73—16172
ISBN 0-670-13369-8

Story/Research Consultant: Charles Hofmann

Without limiting the rights under copyright reserved above, no part of this
publication may be reproduced, stored in or introduced into a retrieval
system, or transmitted, in any form or by any means (electronic, mechanical,
photocopying, recording or otherwise), without the prior written permission
of both the copyright owner and the above publisher of this book.

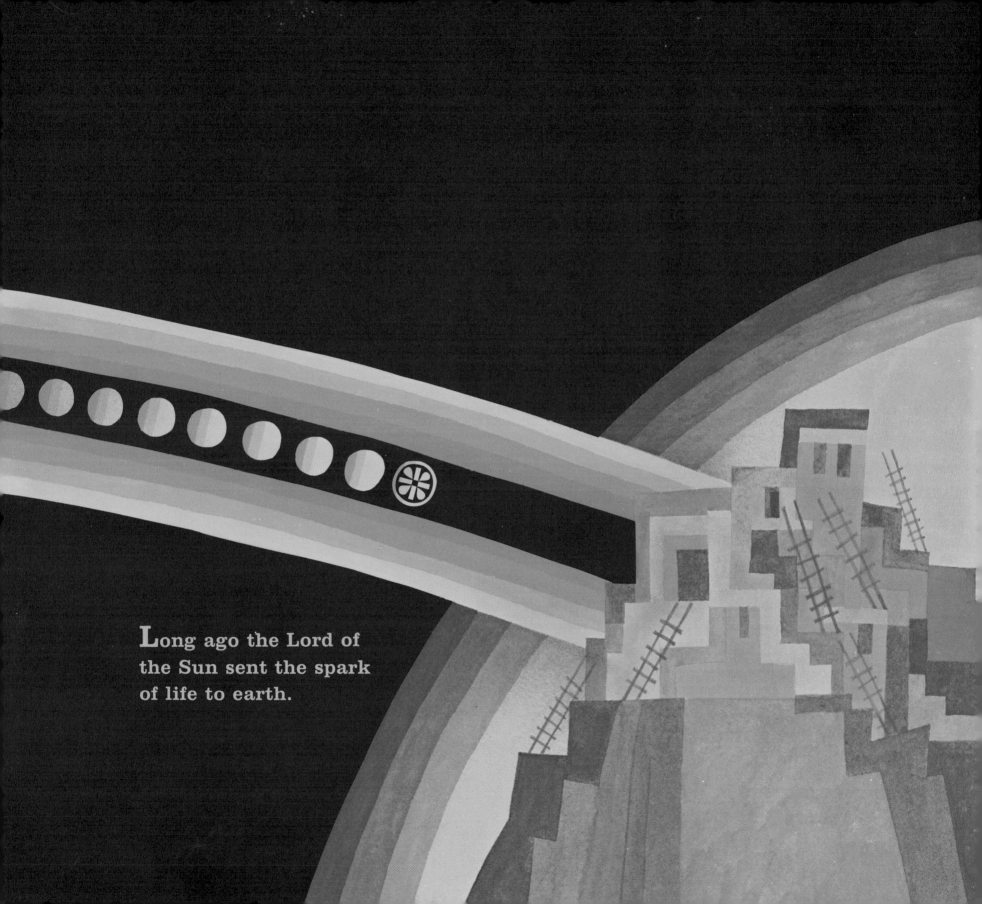

Long ago the Lord of the Sun sent the spark of life to earth.

It traveled down the rays of the sun, through the heavens, and it came to the pueblo. There it entered the house of a young maiden.

In this way, the Boy came into the world of men.

He lived and grew and played in the
pueblo. But the other boys would not
let him join their games. "Where is
your father?" they asked. "You have no
father!" They mocked him and chased
him away. The Boy and his mother
were sad.

"Mother," he said one day, "I must look
for my father. No matter where he is, I
must find him."

So the Boy left home.

He traveled through the world of men
and came to Corn Planter. "Can you
lead me to my father?" he asked. Corn
Planter said nothing, but continued
to tend his crops.

The Boy went to Pot Maker. "Can you
lead me to my father?" asked the Boy.
Pot Maker said nothing, but continued
to make her clay pots.

LINTHICUM ELEMENTARY
SCHOOL LIBRARY

Then the Boy went to Arrow Maker, who was a wise man. "Can you lead me to my father?" Arrow Maker did not answer, but, because he was wise, he saw that the Boy had come from the Sun. So he created a special arrow.

The Boy became the arrow.

Arrow Maker fitted the Boy to his bow and drew it. The Boy flew into the heavens. In this way, the Boy traveled to the sun.

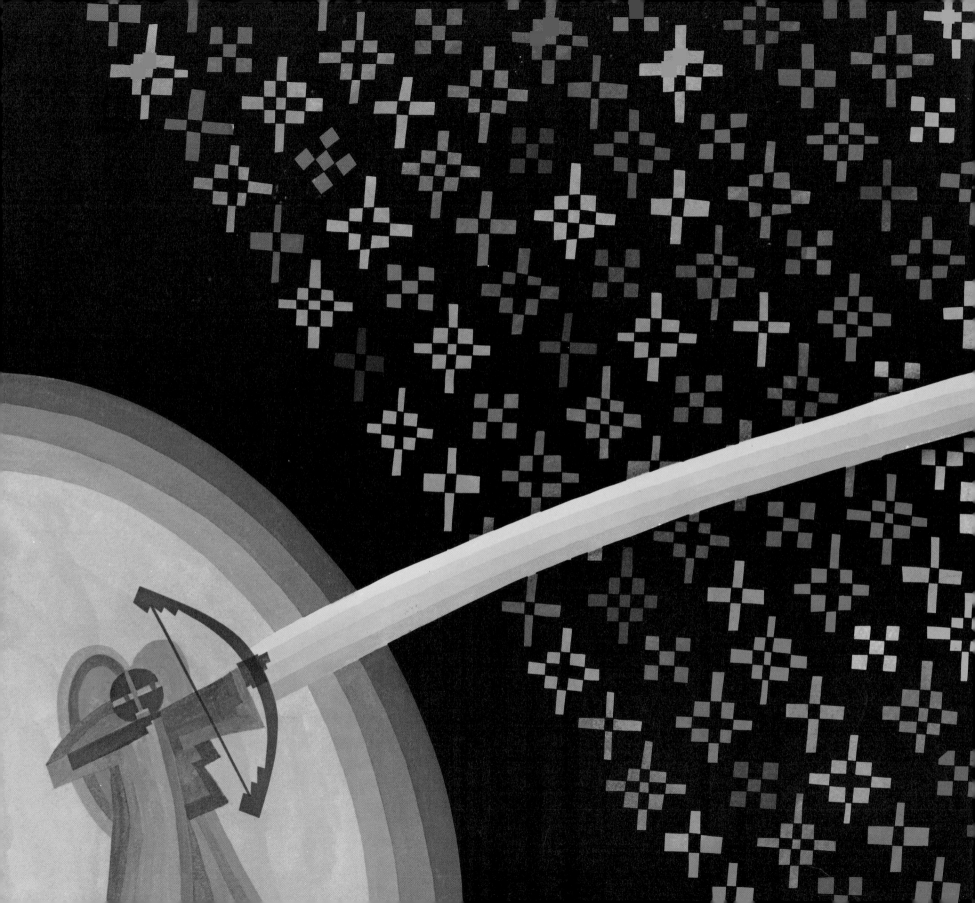

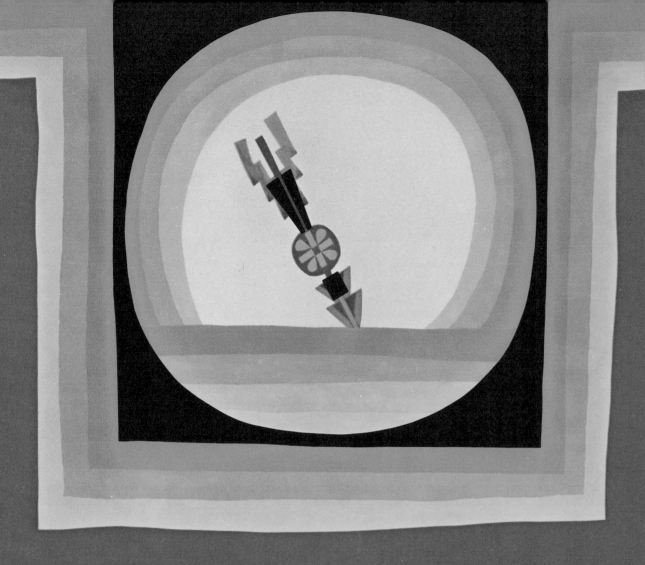

When the Boy saw the mighty Lord, he cried, "Father, it is I, your son!"

"Perhaps you are my son," the Lord replied, "perhaps you are not. You must prove yourself. You must pass through the four chambers of ceremony—the Kiva of Lions, the Kiva of Serpents, the Kiva of Bees, and the Kiva of Lightning."

The Boy was not afraid.
"Father," he said,
"I will endure these trials."

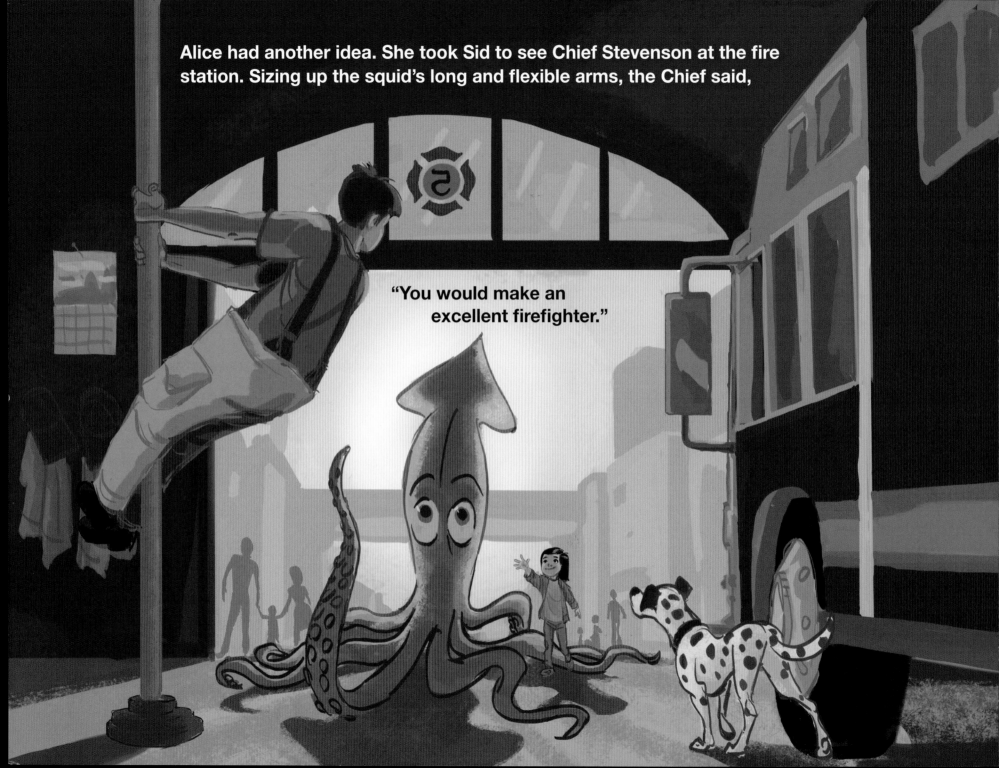

Alice had another idea. She took Sid to see Chief Stevenson at the fire station. Sizing up the squid's long and flexible arms, the Chief said,

"You would make an excellent firefighter."

So Sid became the town's first fire-squid.

Alice and the firemen thought this was a fantastic job for Sid. But he wasn't so sure. Squids need to have wet skin to be happy. Fighting fires was too hot and dry. So Sid and Alice kept looking.

While Sid cooled off in the calm waters by the wharf, Alice saw a restaurant and said, "Aha! Sid, you could be a terrific cook."

Chef Umberto agreed. Sid was amazing!
He could dice carrots, simmer a white sauce, sauté
onions, bake lasagna, and even cook pizzas all at once!
Even Sid thought cooking in the kitchen was the job for him.

That is until someone ordered seafood.

Sid and Alice left the restaurant...but not before releasing all of his new friends into the water.

Finding the perfect job can be tough,
so Alice took Sid to the library.
There Miss Beckstrand, the librarian,
helped them. Searching in books,
magazines, newspapers, and online,
Sid and Alice found lots of new
careers he could try.

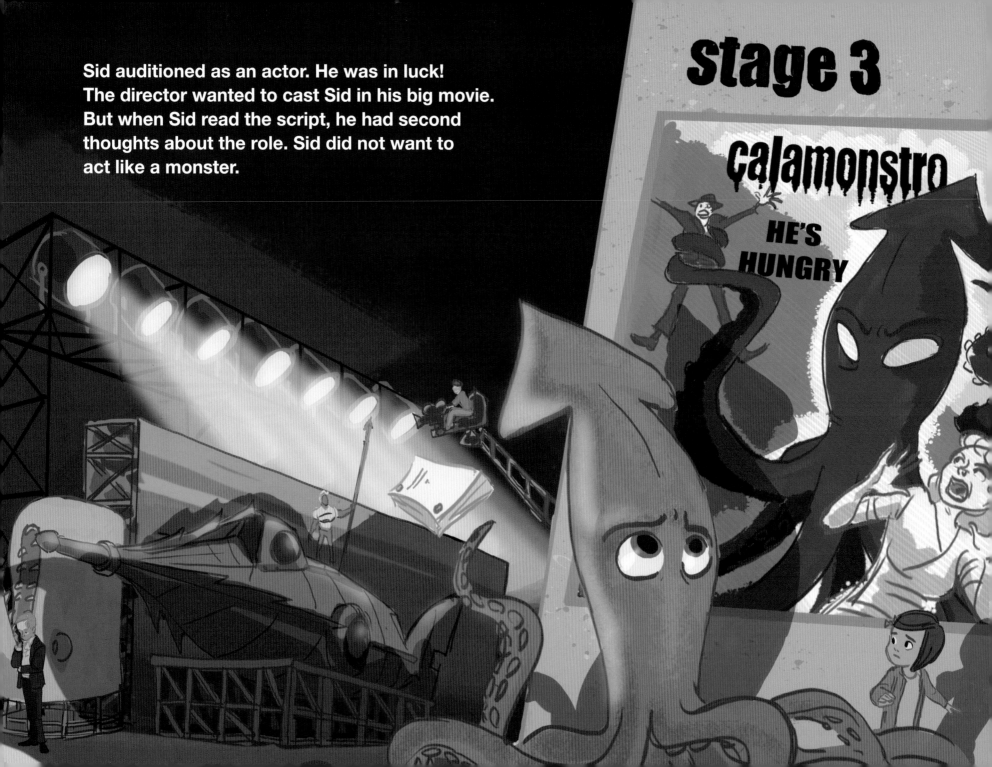

Sid auditioned as an actor. He was in luck! The director wanted to cast Sid in his big movie. But when Sid read the script, he had second thoughts about the role. Sid did not want to act like a monster.

stage 3

calamonstro

HE'S HUNGRY

Next Sid climbed tall buildings to wash windows. Unfortunately, his suction cups made them even dirtier.

Sid walked dogs.

Walking dogs was definitely "knot" the right job.

Sid was a one-squid pit crew...

Ouch!

No matter how hard they tried, they couldn't find Sid the right job. He thought that perhaps it was time to quit the big city and go back home.

Splash!

Sid and Alice jumped up when they heard
the noise. In the distance, they saw an enormous
whale struggling in a net. He needed help!

Instantly Sid swam like
a torpedo out to sea.

Working quickly, Sid used all of his arms
to untangle and free the whale.

The whale thanked Sid by leaping out of the water.
"Sid you were wonderful!" Alice shouted from
a nearby boat. "These people are animal rescuers
who work at the Aquarium." Sid had never
heard of such a place before.

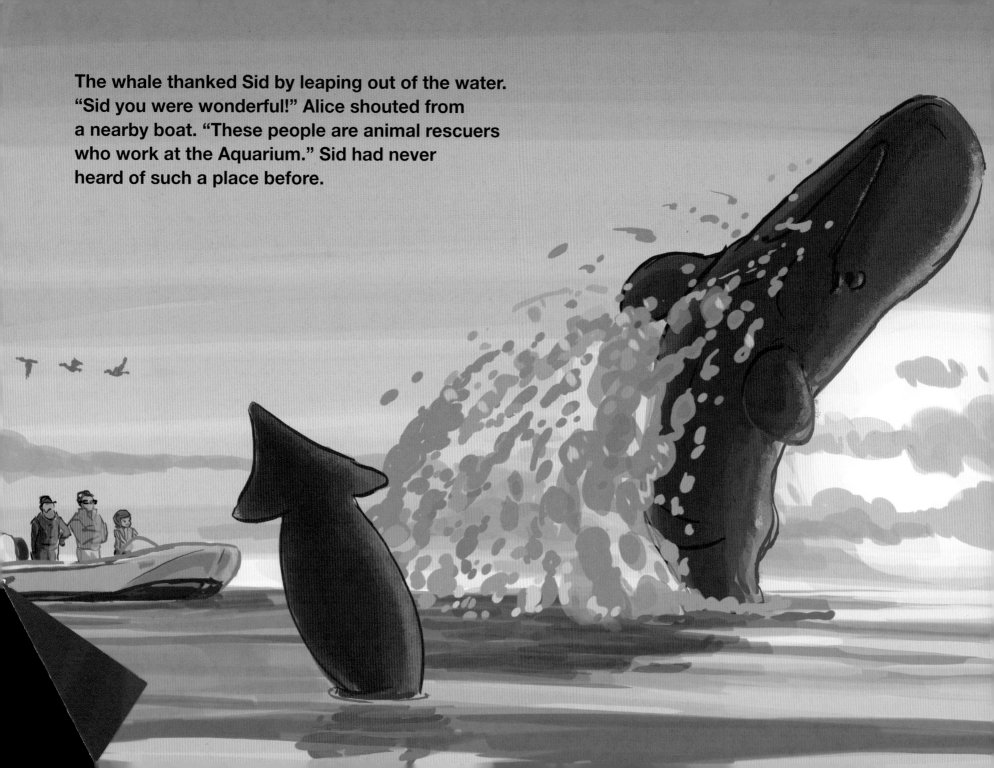

So Alice took him there. "Sid," continued Alice with a big smile, "I think I've found the perfect job for you."

And she did.
The Aquarium was a wonderful place for someone with ten arms.

He could help his aquatic friends
                    great and small and...

teach everyone about his marvelous home, the ocean. So whether you have ten arms like Sid or only two, there is a perfect job out there for everyone. You just have to find it.